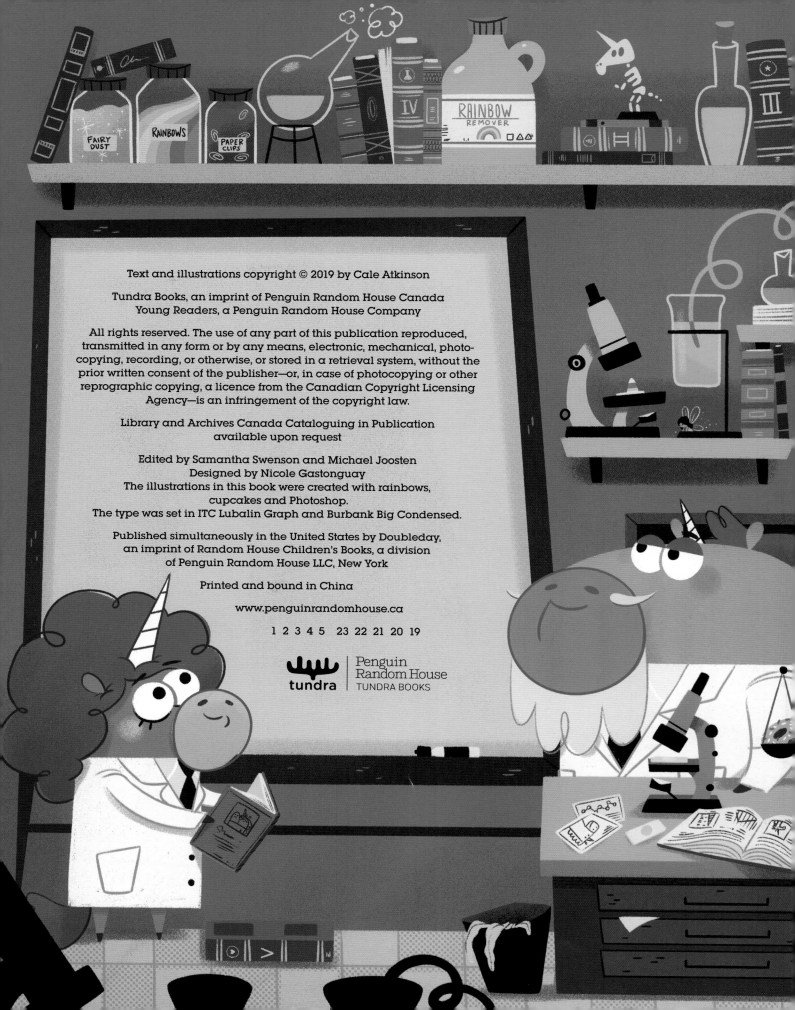

Tundra Books, an imprint of Penguin Random House Canada
Young Readers, a Penguin Random House Company

Library and Archives Canada Cataloguing in Publication
available upon request

Edited by Samantha Swenson and Michael Joosten
Designed by Nicole Gastonguay
The illustrations in this book were created with rainbows,
cupcakes and Photoshop.
The type was set in ITC Lubalin Graph and Burbank Big Condensed.

Published simultaneously in the United States by Doubleday,
an imprint of Random House Children's Books, a division
of Penguin Random House LLC, New York

Printed and bound in China

www.penguinrandomhouse.ca

1 2 3 4 5   23 22 21 20 19

tundra | Penguin
Random House
TUNDRA BOOKS

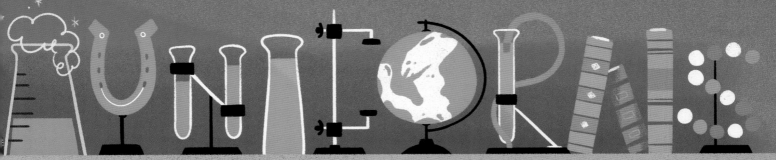

UNICORN

By
Cale Atkinson

UNICORNS

You've seen them. You love them.
But how much do you *really* know about them?

Meet the top unicorn scientists working today!

PROFESSOR GLITTER PANTS

Grand Unistorian

PROFESSOR SPRINKLE STEED

Doctor of Magic

PROFESSOR STAR HOOF

Rainbowmetrics Specialist

PROFESSOR SUGAR BEARD

Certified Hornologist

Pete →

These unicorn masterminds—with the help of their trusty lab assistant, Pete—are here to bring the facts, settle the mysteries, and show us what the deal is with unicorns.

SECTION 1
What Is a Unicorn?

It takes more than a fancy horn to be a unicorn! Using Pete as our example, let's have a closer look at what a unicorn is like.

Common name: Unicorn

Scientific name: *Betterthan horsicus*

Family: MagicaHornidae

Size: Hoof to head, 30–67 hamsters tall

Horn: 4–20 rainbow meters long

Weight: 40,000 gummy bears

Colors: All of them

Group of unicorns: Cornucopia

Name for young: Candycorns

Life span: Super long

Did you know?

You can tell the age of a unicorn by counting the rings on the horn.

SECTION 2
Biology

A unicorn's key features are what separate it from the common horse, typical donkey, or unremarkable pony.

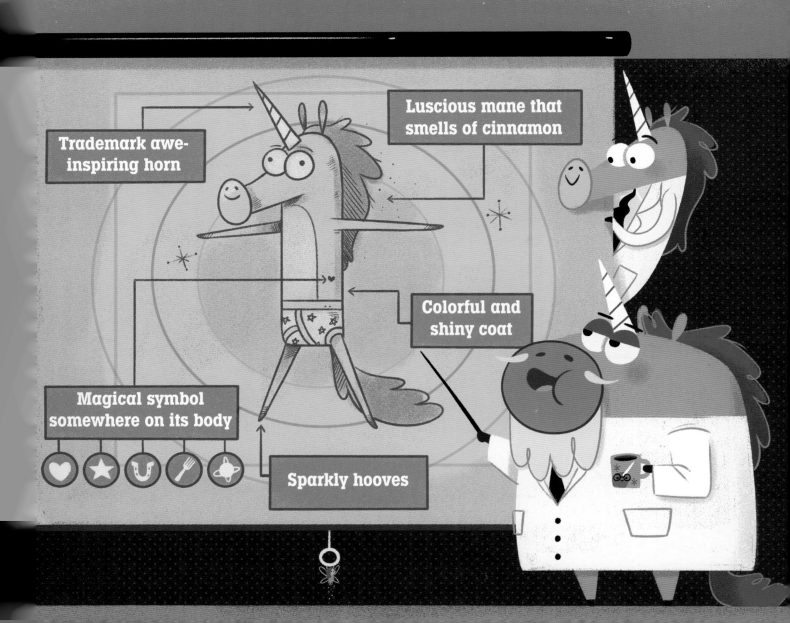

SECTION 3
The Horn of the Corn

Unicorns are known for their legendary horns. Made of 50% magic, 45% mystery, and 5% sugar, unicorn horns are full of unknown and unpredictable powers.

Cases of unicorns accidentally using their horn's power include:

Sparks Sprinkletoot, 1990: Made it rain waffles for a full week.

Peppy Powerhoof, 1982: Made rainbows shoot out of the eyes of a chicken named Gus.

* Doughnut holder
* Tent pole
* Marshmallow stick
* Piñata smasher

SECTION 4
Diet & Digestion

A unicorn's diet is important to keep coats glittery, manes full, and horns strong.

While horses may be happy eating boring old hay, unicorns crave the finer things.

Things unicorns eat:

Ruby-and-emerald flapjacks

24-carat cake

Peanut butter and pixie dust sandwiches

Things unicorns avoid:

Salad bars

Cheese platters

Utensils

In the name of science, we need to cover what happens after a unicorn eats.

Professor Star Hoof, are you sure?!

I'm afraid we must. For science.

Like all other animals, unicorns have to go to the bathroom . . . with one slight difference.

Unicorns poop cupcakes.
Yes. Cupcakes.

BAKE SALE

YUM!

TASTY!

This is why you'll never find a unicorn at a bake sale.

SECTION 5
Unicorn Types

Did you know there are a large variety of unicorns?

They include:

Siberian fur-corn

Miniature-corn

Muscle-corn

Super-horn-corn

Pug-corn

Mustache-corn

As we research and travel, new types are still being discovered.

Rare and exotic unicorns include:

* Zebra-corn
* Koala-corn
* Flamingo-corn
* Mer-corn
* Hamster-corn

Unicorn History

Let's gallop back in time for a brief moment and learn where unicorns came from.

You can see here how, over the past million years, unicorns went from water to land and, eventually, to Pete.

Amoeba-corn

Fish-corn

Amphibian-corn

Lizard-corn

Dino-corn

Ape-corn

Horse-corn

Magesti-corn

Pete

Bird-corn

Fly-corn

Behold! Our gallery of history's most famous unicorns:

DR. HOOF SWEETMANE:
First unicorn to stand
on two legs

**PROFESSOR
SPARKS MOONDUST:**
First unicorn to harness
the power of the rainbow

JOLLY FANCYHOOVES:
First unicorn to wear clothes

BUTTERCUP SPARKLECHEEKS:
First unicorn to trot on Pluto

CAPTAIN CANDYBEARD:
Discoverer of the mer-corn

MONSIEUR BONBON:
First unicorn to
speak French

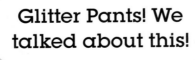

Glitter Pants! We
talked about this!

SECTION 7
Habitat & Homes

Where does a unicorn live?
Let's take a look at Pete's
home to find out!

Three telltale signs you found a unicorn home:

1. Guard'n gnomes
2. Fairy infestation
3. Horn shape in doorway

HANG IN
THERE, BABY!

SECTION 8
Social Behaviors

Social animals by nature, unicorns always enjoy chitchatting about the weather and discussing whose mane is brightest.

Favorite unicorn activities include:

Horn jousting

Competitive ringtoss

Javelin throwing

Knitting circles

But unicorns have a much more civilized way of solving disagreements:

the ancient ritual of **the dance-off!**

Common Unicorn Questions

Why don't I ever see a unicorn?

Unicorns have become masters of disguise, in order to live a normal life and avoid being mobbed by "cornies" everywhere they go.

See if you can spot Pete hiding in these examples.

What does a baby unicorn look like?

There's a reason why you don't see baby unicorns. They are too cute. Well, not just "too cute." They are cuteness overload. Many people have been forever changed by the high level of cuteness!

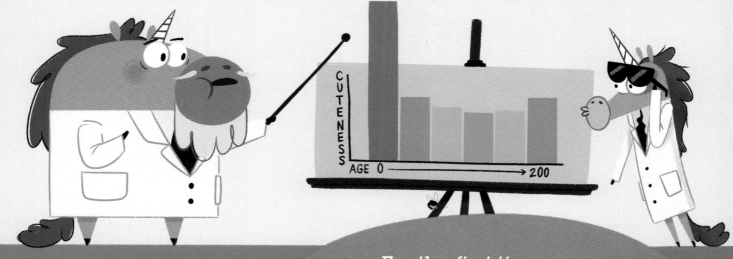

For the first time ever, we will give you a glimpse of a baby unicorn. *But be warned.* Stare too long, and you'll be seeing nothing but glitter for the next week. Prepare your peepers, 'cause here we go. . . .

Is it true that unicorns are the most magical creatures in existence?

Yes. Obviously. As well as the most majestic, magnificent, and cool. Other notable magical creatures include pixies, corgis, and wizard yaks.

What do unicorns use rainbows for?

The REAL question is, what DON'T unicorns use rainbows for? They paint their homes with rainbows, fuel their cars with rainbows, and even flavor their pancakes with rainbows! If you see a rainbow, you can bet your horn there's a unicorn nearby!

SECTION 10
Graduation Celebration!

CONGRATULATIONS! By completing this book and learning all the juicy unicorn knowledge, you have earned your white lab coat and now join the ranks of brilliant unicorn scientists! Welcome to the team!

Maybe you'll be the one to discover the next rare unicorn!

Unicornius Scientificus

Diploma

successfully finished this course
and earned the prestigious title of

Unicorn Scientist

Go forth and be proud, knowing that you are
one of the majestic, the magical, the super rad.

Professor Glitter Pants

Professor Star Hoof

Professor Sprinkle Steed

Professor Sugar Beard

*This document is 100% legitimate in the eyes of all unicorns.

This book
belongs to

Emmaconner

Why Is The Sky Blue?

* Discover why the sky changes color

* Find out what air is made from

* Learn about rainbows and sunsets

Have you ever wondered why the sky is blue and why it is sometimes other colors too?

We live on a planet called Earth. There is a layer of air around it called the atmosphere. When you look up you can see it high above you. This is what we call the sky.

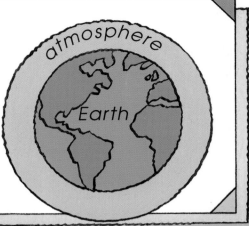

3

The Sun is far away in space. It is a glowing ball of fire. The Sun shines very brightly. The light it sends out travels through space to Earth.

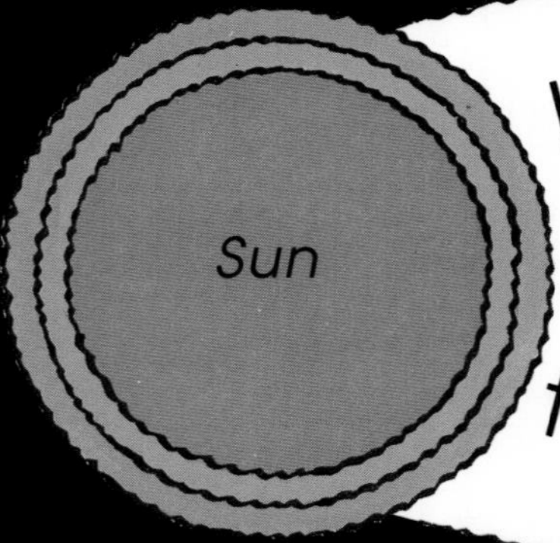

Sun

Imagine that the sunlight shines like a flashlight through the darkness.

This picture shows sunlight traveling to Earth through black space.

4

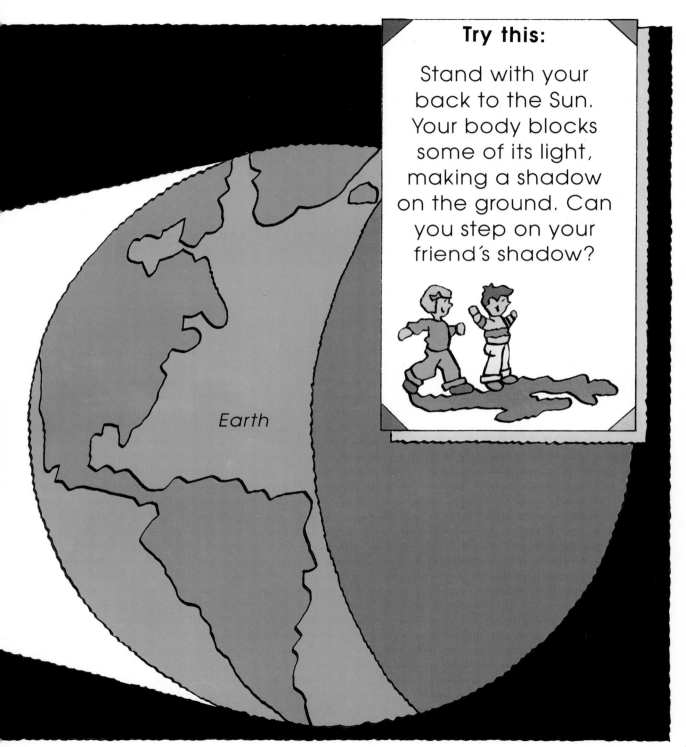

Try this:

Stand with your back to the Sun. Your body blocks some of its light, making a shadow on the ground. Can you step on your friend's shadow?

Earth

On Earth, the sunlight fills the sky. In summer, the sky is often blue. Sometimes there are fluffy white clouds.

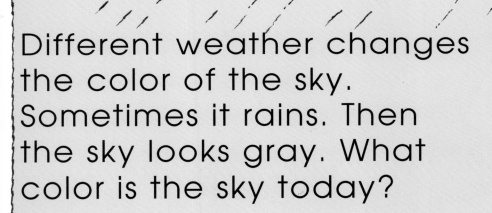

Different weather changes the color of the sky. Sometimes it rains. Then the sky looks gray. What color is the sky today?

Try this:

Keep a sky color journal. Every day paint a new page the colors of that day's sky.

What color do you think sunlight is? It might be a surprise, but it is made of seven different colors!

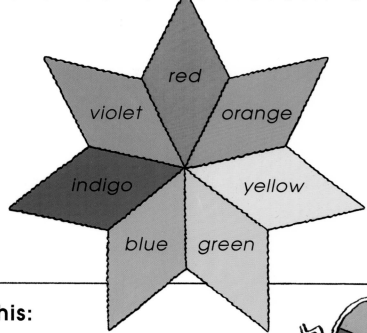

Try this:

Divide a card circle into seven sections. Lightly color them in as shown. Thread string through. Hold the ends and swing the circle around. Pull the string tight so it spins fast. Watch the colors blend together until they look almost white.

Sunlight usually looks clear, but when there is a rainbow you can see all the colors. Rainbows form when the Sun shines through raindrops. The raindrops split the light into its seven different colors.

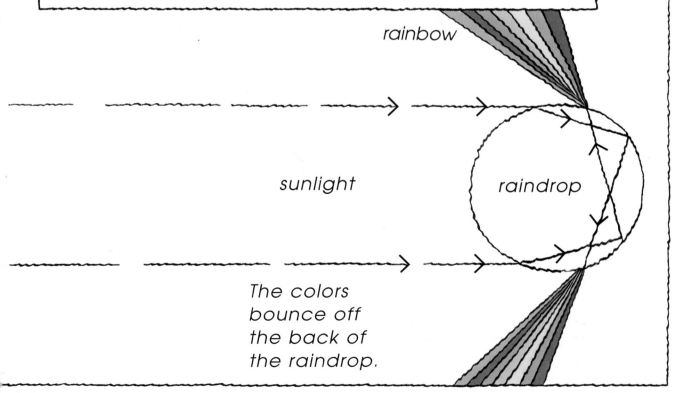

rainbow

sunlight

raindrop

The colors bounce off the back of the raindrop.

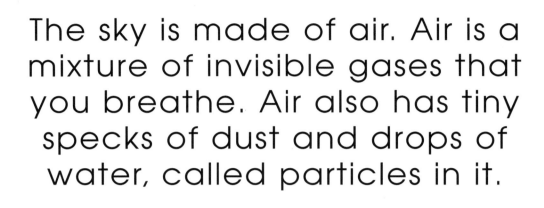

The sky is made of air. Air is a mixture of invisible gases that you breathe. Air also has tiny specks of dust and drops of water, called particles in it.

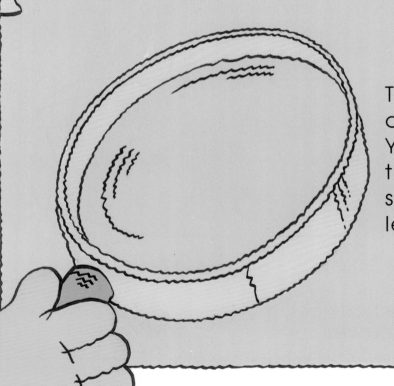

The particles are nearly invisible. You cannot see them, even with a strong magnifying lens.

Try this:

On a sunny day, stand near a window and look at the rays of sunlight coming into the room. Can you see dust floating in the sunlight? These are like the tiny particles that fill the sky.

dust

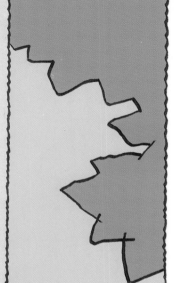

Sun

When sunlight passes through the sky it hits the floating particles and bounces in all directions.

More of the blue light is scattered than any other color.

That's why the sky looks blue!

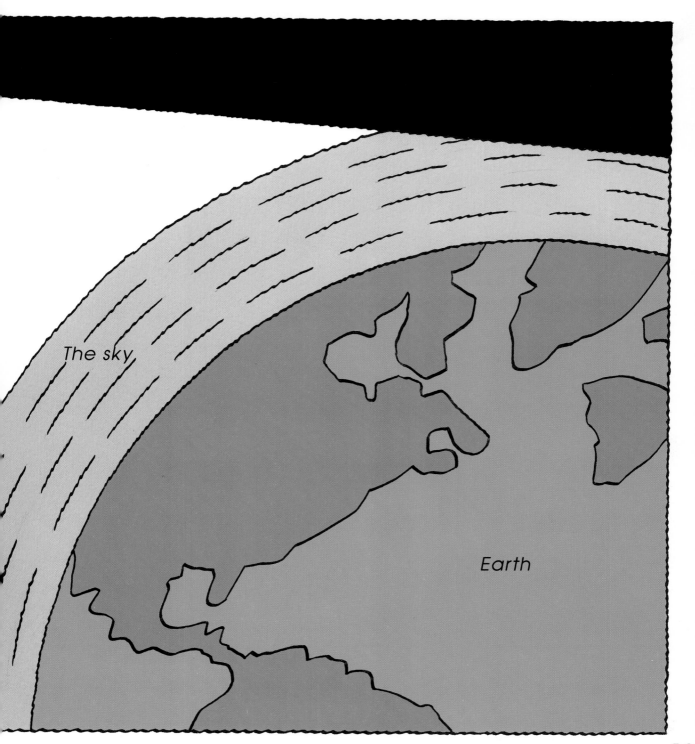

The sky

Earth

Sometimes it is misty and clouds cover up the sky. They stop the sunlight shining through.

Make some blindfolds out of dark-colored materials and light-colored materials. Which material blocks out the light best? Do dark-colored materials block out the light more than light-colored ones?

white cotton

silky scarf

dark cotton   *red material*

The world becomes dark and gloomy.

The Earth turns in space.
When one side of the Earth
is facing away from the Sun it
is night. The sky is black.
Sunlight is filling the sky on the
other side of the planet.

Try this:

Find a dark room and shine a flashlight onto a ball. This is like the Sun shining on the Earth. One side of the ball is light and the other is dark. The Sun makes day and night on the Earth in the same way.

As the day begins or ends, the color of the sky changes. On a clear day, as the Sun goes down, it might even be orange. This is called a sunset.

The Sun is high in the sky at midday. Its light travels down toward the Earth. At sunset the Sun is low in the sky. You see it through a thicker layer of air that makes the light look orange.

midday

Earth

sunset

Earth

Try this:

Make a sunset picture. Cut out colored tissue paper shapes. Glue them onto a sheet of paper.

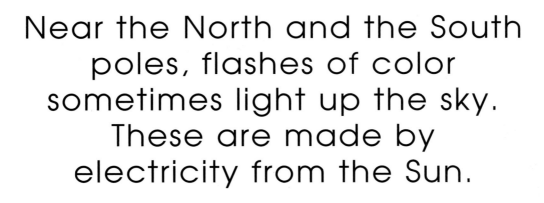

Near the North and the South poles, flashes of color sometimes light up the sky. These are made by electricity from the Sun.

The Sun's electricity crashes into particles in the air making strange and fantastic colors.

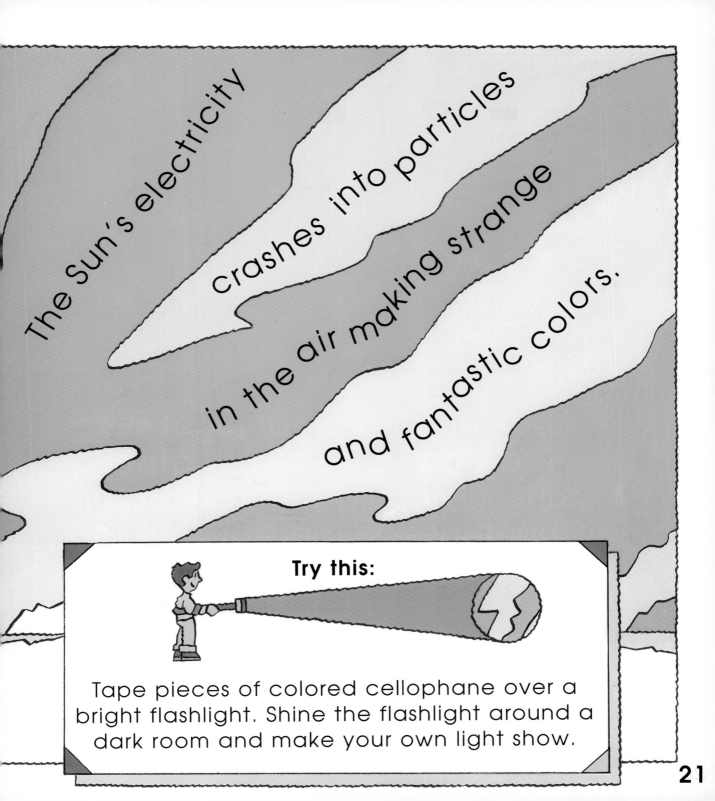

Try this:

Tape pieces of colored cellophane over a bright flashlight. Shine the flashlight around a dark room and make your own light show.

Look up at a clear night sky.
The stars you see are other
suns, giving light to millions of
other planets. The stars are too
far away to give much light
to Earth.

The planet Mars is Earth's closest neighbor. Light from the Sun reaches Mars, but the sky is a reddish color. This is because Mars has no air — only dust particles that make the sky look red.

DID YOU KNOW?

Scientists who study the weather are called meteorologists. They figure out what the weather will be like.

Meteorologists work in weather stations. They study the sky and look at the different weather around the world.

Information is collected by special weather ships, by weather balloons, and by space satellites. The information is sent to the weather stations.

The longest-lasting rainbow ever seen stayed in the sky for over three hours.

Many people believe that when the sky is red in the evening, the weather next day will be good.

The sunniest place in the world is in Arizona. The sun shines here almost every day.

At the South Pole there are 182 days of darkness each year when the sun does not shine.

Why Does It Rain?

* Find out why it rains

* Discover how clouds are made

* Learn about thunder and lightning

Sometimes it rains. Water comes pouring down out of the sky and soaks the ground.

26

Try this:

rainy

sunny

windy

snowy

Make a weather chart.
Each day, draw a shape
on it to show whether
it is raining or sunny,
snowing or windy.

The rain makes everything wet.

Rain gives us water. People need water to keep them alive. Animals also need water. Trees and plants soak up rainwater through their roots.

root

Try this:

Put a piece of celery in a glass of colored water. Can you see how the color rises up the celery as it soaks up the water? In the same way, plants use their roots to drink water from the ground.

In some parts of the world very little rain falls. These places are called deserts. Only a few special plants and animals can live here, as there is hardly any water.

Try this:

Plant some seeds in two containers of soil. Keep them in the same place for a week, but water only one container. Which seeds do you think will grow best?

When there is too much rain, rivers can overflow. Water pours onto the land in a flood. Where does all this rain come from?

Try this:

Go outside and put some soil on a tray. Stick some twigs into the soil. Now pour a jug of water over the tray. Watch everything get washed away in your own flood!

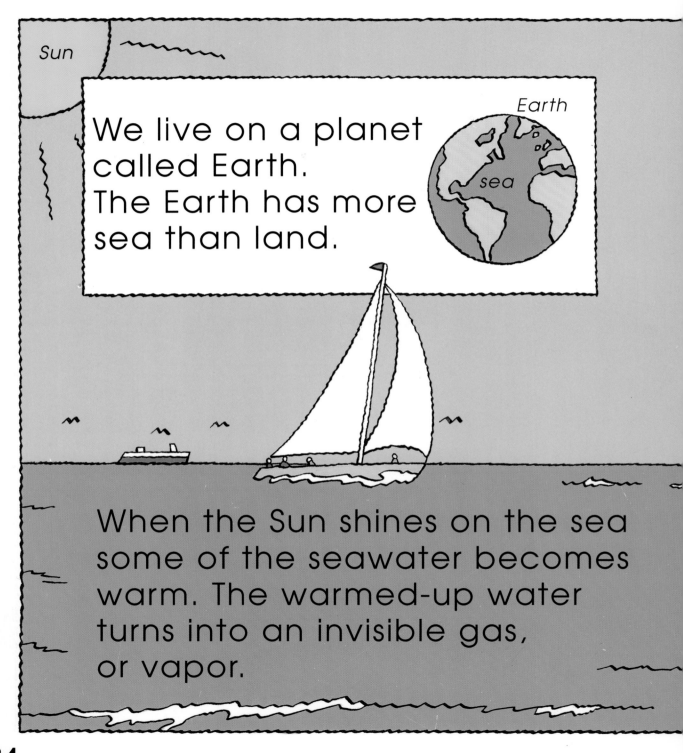

Sun

We live on a planet called Earth.
The Earth has more sea than land.

Earth

sea

When the Sun shines on the sea some of the seawater becomes warm. The warmed-up water turns into an invisible gas, or vapor.

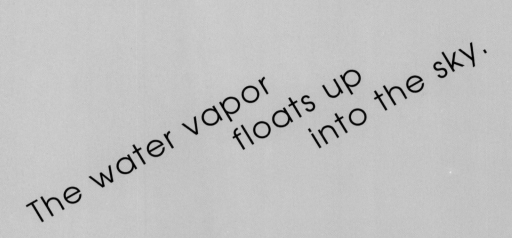

The water vapor floats up into the sky.

sea

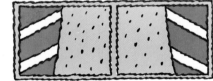

Try this:

When laundry dries, the water in it becomes vapor. Next time laundry is drying indoors, look for water drops on the windows. The vapor cools on the cold glass and turns back into water.

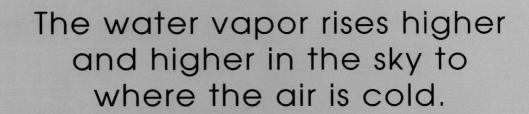

The water vapor rises higher
and higher in the sky to
where the air is cold.

cloud

When the vapor gets cold it turns back into little drops of water. These make clouds.

Try this:

Look at the sky on a cloudy day. Can you see any pictures in the clouds? Paint the shapes you see. Dab cotton balls dipped in watery paint onto a sheet of paper.

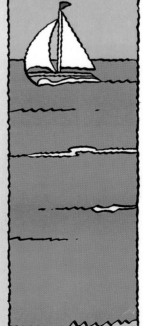

cirrus

stratus

cumulus

stratus

Try this:

Look for different kinds of clouds. Cirrus — wispy, high clouds — mean rain or snow. Cumulus — fluffy, piled-up clouds — can mean showers. Stratus — a thick blanket of cloud — can fill the air with damp drizzle.

It is raining.

Try this:

See how much rain falls in a week. Cut off the top of a plastic bottle. Dig a shallow hole in the ground and place the bottle in it. Each day, mark the level of rainwater on the bottle.

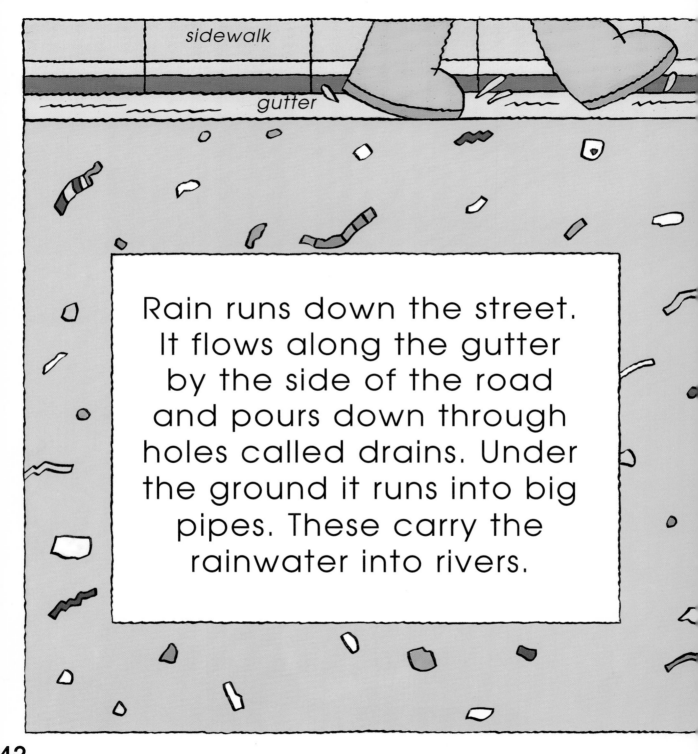

sidewalk

gutter

Rain runs down the street. It flows along the gutter by the side of the road and pours down through holes called drains. Under the ground it runs into big pipes. These carry the rainwater into rivers.

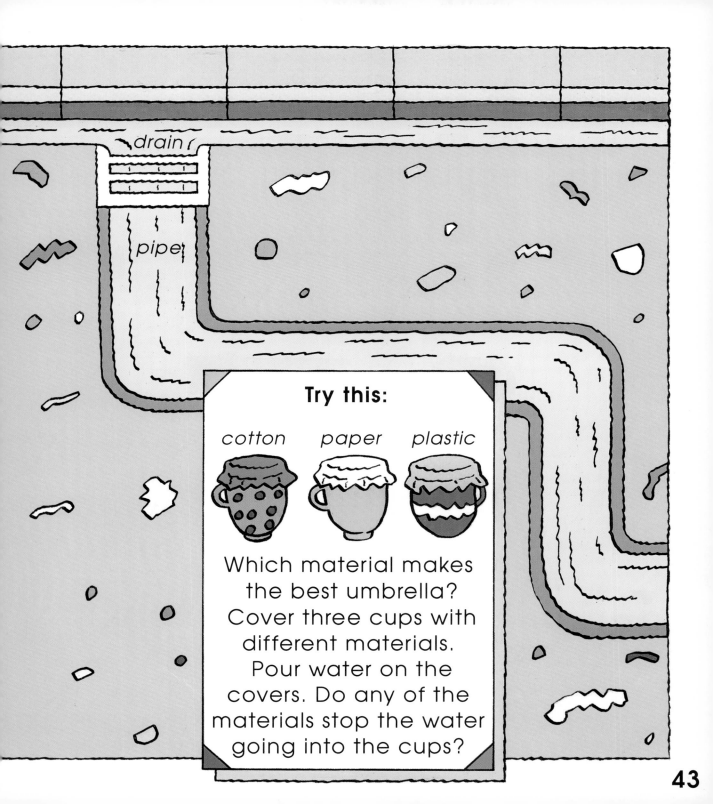

drain

pipe

Try this:

cotton   *paper*   *plastic*

Which material makes
the best umbrella?
Cover three cups with
different materials.
Pour water on the
covers. Do any of the
materials stop the water
going into the cups?

In the countryside, rain falls onto the mountains and hills. It flows into streams and rivers and along to the sea.

Try this:

After it has rained, find a
puddle and draw around
it with chalk. Wait for an
hour and draw around it
again. How long does it
take for the puddle to
dry up completely?

45

The rivers flow down to the sea.

Now the rainwater is back in the sea. When the Sun warms the seawater, more water vapor will rise into the sky. It will make a new cloud and somewhere it will soon start to rain...

Try this:

splash

splosh

Half fill a plastic bottle with water. Screw the lid on tightly and shake the bottle to make heavy rain noises. Now, pat your legs to make the sound of gentle rain. What other rain sounds can you make?

47

DID YOU KNOW?

People first began to keep scientific records of the weather about 160 years ago.

Meteorologists figure out how much rain falls each day by collecting rain in a special container. The rain is then poured into a measuring cylinder.

In 1952, on Reunion Island in the Indian Ocean, 73 inches of rain fell in just 24 hours!

The wettest place on Earth is in Colombia, South America.

The driest place on Earth is a part of Chile, South America. Less than 0.004 inch of rain falls here each year.

In 1971, part of the Atacama Desert, in Peru, had its first rainfall in 400 years.

Mawsynram, in India, is one of the wettest places in the world. Each year it has over 45 inches of rain.

Some very strange downpours have been seen in some places — of frogs, snakes, mice, and even of money!

Why Is It Cold Today?

* Find out what makes the weather cold

* Learn how snow is made

* Discover why it is cold in winter

Is it cold today?
When it is very cold you can
see frost on the ground.

Sometimes
snow
falls
from
the
sky.

50

The frost makes fern shapes.

Try this:

Pour warm water into
a dish and cover it
with a clear plate.
Put the dish in the freezer.
After a few hours, take
out the plate. Little drops
of water will have frozen
on it and made frost.

Ponds and lakes turn to ice.

51

Snow forms high up in the air. It is made of tiny ice crystals. The ice crystals join together to make snowflakes that fall to the ground.

ice crystals

When snow covers the ground it acts like a blanket. It stops heat escaping and keeps the soil from freezing.

Try this:

See how much space snow takes up. Find two jars exactly the same size. Fill one up with water. Fill the other with snow, or use frost from the freezer. Wait for the snow to melt. What do you notice?

When you feel cold you shiver.
Sometimes your teeth chatter.
You can see your warm breath
like smoke in the cold air.

In cold weather, people wear thick clothes to keep warm. Animals grow thick fur to keep out the cold.

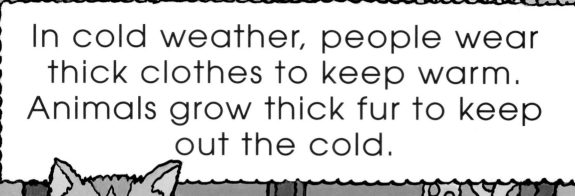

Try this:

Find some clothes you wear when it is cold. Find some clothes for when it is hot. Choose a piece of clothing from each pile. Wrap one around each hand. Which hand is warmer? Which clothes keep you warmest?

T-shirt

wool scarf

It is cold in winter. This is
one of the four seasons.
The seasons after winter
are spring, summer, and fall.

Try this:

Put out food and water for the birds that stay behind in winter. You can buy wild birdseed or put out pieces of bread, apple, or bacon. How many different kinds of birds visit your yard each day?

burrow

In winter some animals hide away from the cold in warm burrows. Many birds fly away to warm countries.

The seasons happen as the Earth moves in a circle around the Sun. The Sun's strongest rays shine on different parts of the Earth as it goes around. It takes one year for the Earth to circle the Sun once.

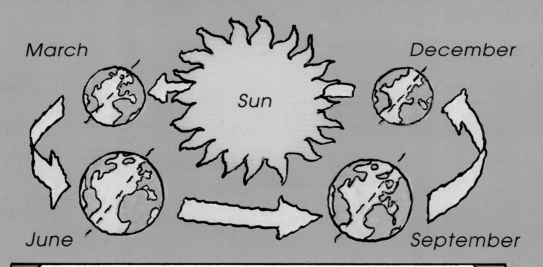

March

December

Sun

June

September

Try this:

Close your eyes and turn your face to the Sun. Does it feel warm? Is the top of your head cooler than your face? It is like summer on your face and winter on your head.

The axis is an imaginary line through the center of the Earth. The axis is tilted, so the Earth leans over as it travels around the Sun.

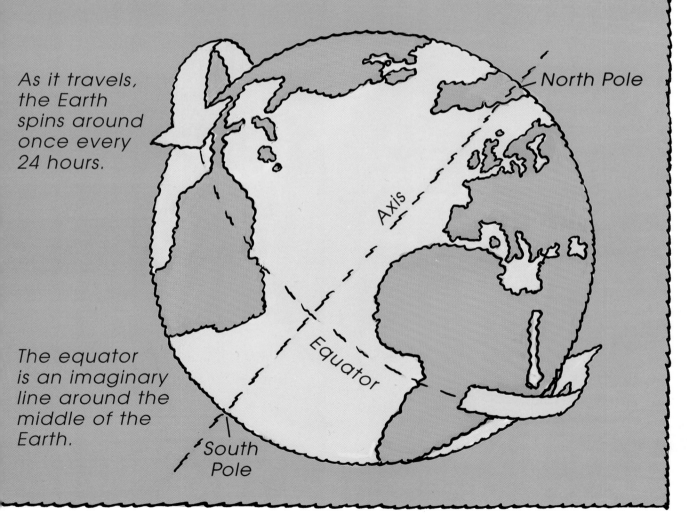

As it travels, the Earth spins around once every 24 hours.

The equator is an imaginary line around the middle of the Earth.

North Pole

Axis

Equator

South Pole

When the North Pole tilts toward the Sun, it is summer in the top half of the Earth, or Northern Hemisphere.

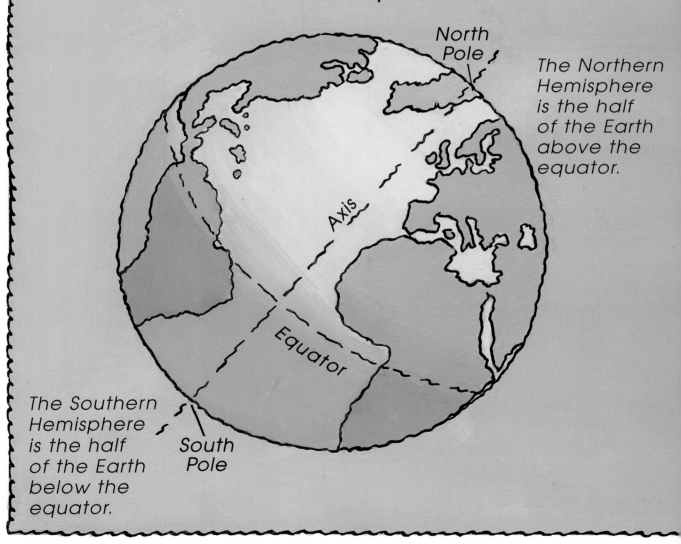

North Pole

The Northern Hemisphere is the half of the Earth above the equator.

Axis

Equator

The Southern Hemisphere is the half of the Earth below the equator.

South Pole

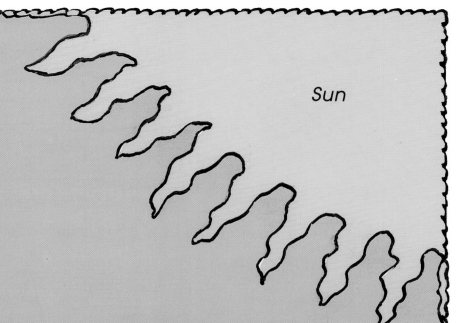

Sun

When the South Pole tilts toward the Sun, it is summer in the bottom half of the Earth, or Southern Hemisphere.

Try this:

Divide a large circle into four sections, spring, summer, fall, and winter. In each section draw a picture of what you like to do best in each season.

winter   spring

fall   summer

Australia and the United States are on opposite halves of the Earth. It is summer in Australia when it is winter in the United States. In Australia, people can spend Christmas Day at the beach.

Try this:

Look for Australia and the United States on a globe. Now look for other countries. Are they in the Northern Hemisphere, or in the Southern Hemisphere? In the top or bottom half of the globe?

The season that comes after winter is spring. It happens in the parts of the Earth that are slowly turning toward the Sun's strongest rays.

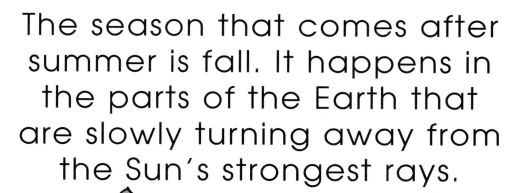

The season that comes after summer is fall. It happens in the parts of the Earth that are slowly turning away from the Sun's strongest rays.

Try this:

Collect some fallen leaves. Lay them between two pieces of paper. Put the paper in a pile of heavy books. Wait for a week, then glue the pressed leaves onto pieces of card.

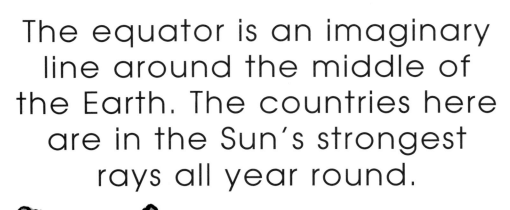

The equator is an imaginary line around the middle of the Earth. The countries here are in the Sun's strongest rays all year round.

Try this:

Fruit often has labels to show where it comes from. Next time you go shopping, make a list of fruit from hot countries. Can you think why fruit from hot countries would not grow well in cold countries?

The Sun's strongest rays never land on the North and South Poles. These parts of the Earth are always cold. They are so cold that some of the sea freezes and makes giant pieces of ice called icebergs.

Try this:

Make a small iceberg. Fill a balloon with water and leave it in the freezer for 24 hours. Take it out and peel away the balloon to leave a large piece of ice. Put it in a bowl of water. Does it float? How much of it is under the water?

The South Pole, or Antarctic, is the coldest place on Earth. Even in the middle of summer the temperature is below freezing.

The only people who live here are scientists. In the sea there are fish, whales, seals, and penguins.

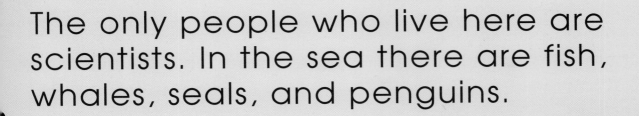

Try this:

Find 3 empty yogurt containers. Put an ice cube in each. Leave one container in the refrigerator, one near a radiator or in sunlight, and one in the middle of the room. Which ice cube takes longest to melt? Can you think why?

DID YOU KNOW?

Meteorologists use different instruments to study the weather.

A thermometer measures temperature (how hot or cold it is) in measurements called degrees Fahrenheit (°F).

A sunshine recorder has a huge glass ball to receive the Sun's rays. It measures how many hours of sunshine there are in a day.

The coldest place on Earth is in the Antarctic. It has a temperature of only -72°F.

One of the hottest places on Earth is Death Valley in California. It is sometimes hotter than 120°F.

An anemometer has three cups that spin around in the wind and a dial to show its speed.

The fastest ever tornado reached a speed of 280 miles per hour!

Why Does The Wind Blow?

* Discover what makes the wind blow

* Find out about the strongest winds

* Learn why it is windy at the beach

On a windy day your hair blows around. Laundry flaps in the wind. Sometimes the wind whistles down chimneys or howls around the corners of houses.

Try this:

Keep a windy weather journal. Hang ribbons or strips of material from a string in the yard. Look at them every day and draw what you see.

No wind: ribbons hang down

Some wind: ribbons blow a little

Windy: ribbons blow around a lot

Very windy: ribbons almost blow away

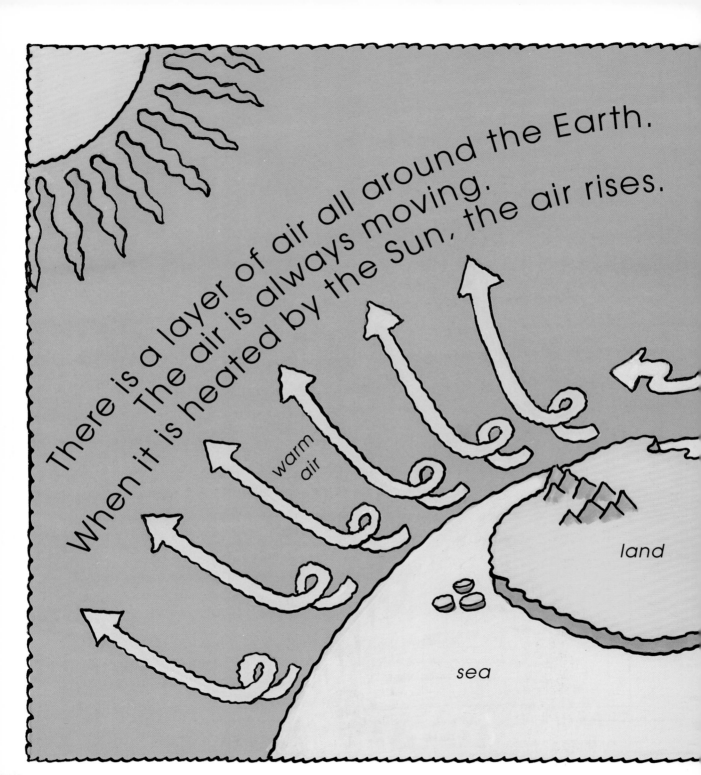

There is a layer of air all around the Earth.
The air is always moving.
When it is heated by the Sun, the air rises.

warm air

land

sea

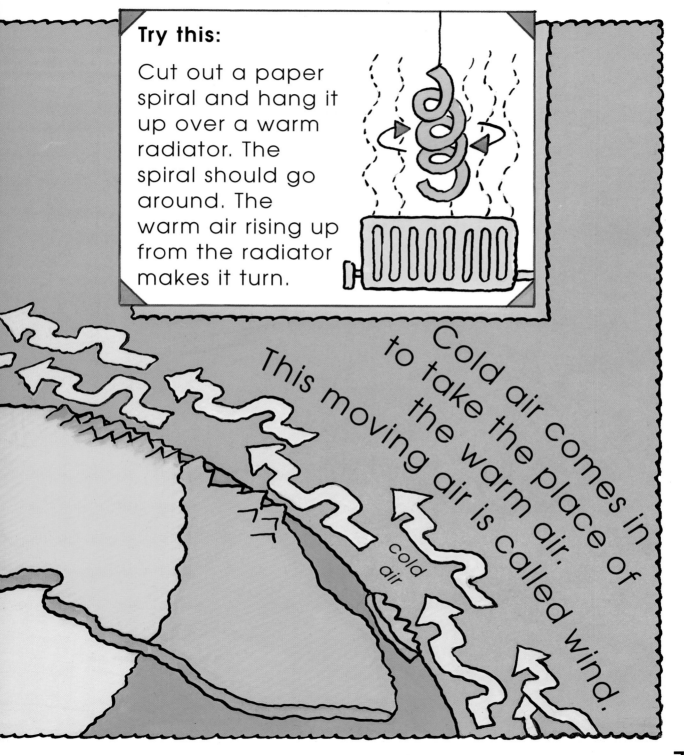

Try this:

Cut out a paper spiral and hang it up over a warm radiator. The spiral should go around. The warm air rising up from the radiator makes it turn.

Cold air comes in to take the place of the warm air. This moving air is called wind.

cold air

The wind can be a gentle breeze. But when warm air rises quickly, cold air rushes in to take its place. Then the wind can be a strong gale.

Try this:

Put blobs of runny paint onto a piece of paper. Blow gently at them through a drinking straw.

In some places it is always windy. At the beach, cool sea breezes blow onto the land. They come in to take the place of the air that is rising from the warm land.

Try this:

Make a paper pinwheel.

1. Fold a square of thin card into a triangle. Fold the triangle in half.

2. Open out the card. Cut along the fold lines to $^1/_2$ inch from the center.

3. Bend over four corners into the center and push through a thumb tack.

Push the tack into a cork. Blow the sails to make them go around.

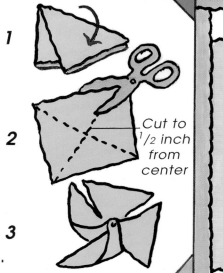

1

2 Cut to $^1/_2$ inch from center

3

81

When wind blows against a hill or cliff it gets pushed upward. Birds like to hover and soar in the sky on these rising airstreams.

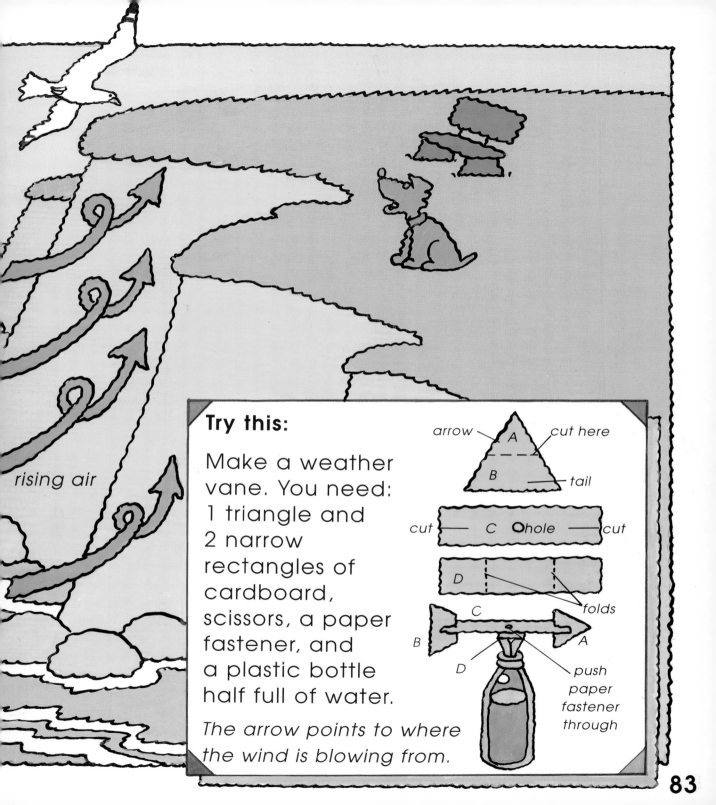

rising air

Try this:

Make a weather vane. You need: 1 triangle and 2 narrow rectangles of cardboard, scissors, a paper fastener, and a plastic bottle half full of water.

The arrow points to where the wind is blowing from.

arrow — A — cut here

B — tail

cut — C ⊙hole — cut

D — folds

C — A

B — D — push paper fastener through

One type of strong
wind is called
a hurricane.
This is a wind that
travels very fast and
causes a lot of
damage. It can blow
over big trees and
even knock down
buildings.

Try this:

Make hurricane sounds on a tape recorder. Blow and whistle into the microphone, bang a tray with a spoon, and shake dried beans in a can for rain sounds.

85

In some parts of the world, a powerful wind called a tornado sometimes blows. A tornado spins around very fast. It pulls up heavy objects into the air.

Try this:

Run water into a sink. Pull out the plug and watch the water drain. It makes a spiral cone shape. This is the same shape as a tornado.

In a hot desert, the wind blows dust and sand up from the ground into the air. It makes a huge sandstorm cloud that blows along.

Try this:

Draw a desert scene. Spread glue on the sandy areas. Shake over real sand, dried rice, or glitter.

89

For centuries, the wind has been used to blow ships across the sea and to turn the sails of windmills.

Try this:

Make a boat. Push
a pencil through a
square of paper.
Use modeling
clay to attach
the pencil into
an empty
margarine tub.
Put the boat in
the bathtub.
Blow into the sail.

91

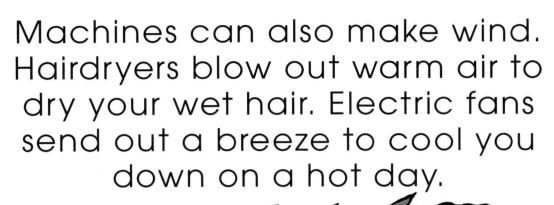

Machines can also make wind. Hairdryers blow out warm air to dry your wet hair. Electric fans send out a breeze to cool you down on a hot day.

Try this:

Make a fan to keep you cool. Draw a pattern on a sheet of paper. Make a narrow fold down one side. Turn the paper over and fold again. When the whole sheet is folded, hold one end and open out the fan.

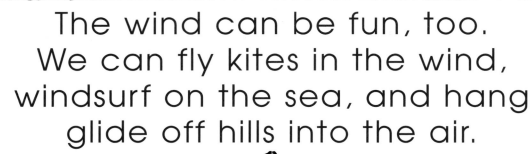

The wind can be fun, too.
We can fly kites in the wind,
windsurf on the sea, and hang
glide off hills into the air.

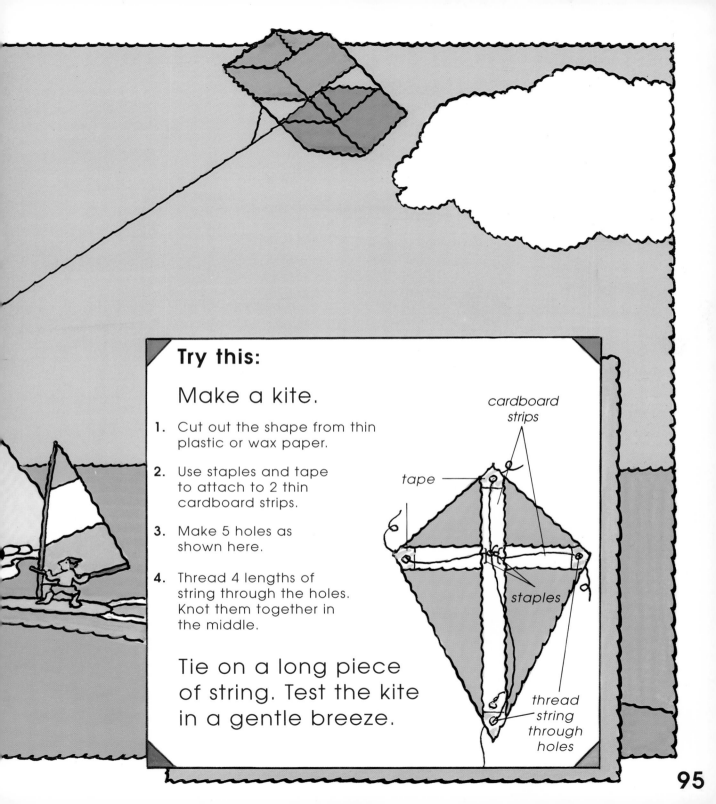

Try this:

Make a kite.

1. Cut out the shape from thin plastic or wax paper.

2. Use staples and tape to attach to 2 thin cardboard strips.

3. Make 5 holes as shown here.

4. Thread 4 lengths of string through the holes. Knot them together in the middle.

Tie on a long piece of string. Test the kite in a gentle breeze.

cardboard strips

tape

staples

thread string through holes

INDEX

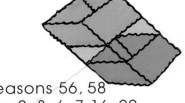

Produced by Zigzag Publishing, <None>a division of Quadrillion Publishing Ltd., Godalming Business Centre, Woolsack Way, Godalming, Surrey GU7 1XW England.

Editors: Janet De Saulles and Hazel Songhurst
Designer: Ross Thomson
IllustratorsL Tony Wells and Robin Lawrie
Concept: Tony Potter

Color separations: Scan Trans, Singapore
Printed in Singapore

This edition distributed in the U.S. by SMITHMARK PUBLISHERS a division of U.S. Media Holdings, Inc.
16 East 32nd Street, New York, NY 10016

Copyright © 1997 Zigzag Publishing
First published in 1993 by Zigzag Publishing

ISBN 0-7651-9339-6

8425